VIKING
ADVENTURES

BITRA
AND THE WITCH

Written and Illustrated by Andy Elkerton

W
FRANKLIN WATTS
LONDON · SYDNEY

Franklin Watts
First published in Great Britain in 2017 by
The Watts Publishing Group

Text and Illustrations © Andy Elkerton 2017

The rights of Andy Elkerton to be identified
as the author and illustrator of this Work
have been asserted in accordance with the
Copyright, Designs and Patents Act, 1988.

Series Editor: Melanie Palmer
Series Designers: Peter Scoulding
and Cathryn Gilbert

ISBN 978 1 4451 5840 2 (hbk)
ISBN 978 1 4451 5841 9 (pbk)

Printed in China

Franklin Watts
An imprint of
Hachette Children's Group
Part of The Watts Publishing Group
Carmelite House
50 Victoria Embankment
London EC4Y 0DZ

An Hachette UK Company
www.hachette.co.uk

www.franklinwatts.co.uk

Chapter One

When the the pot of soup bubbling in the fireplace suddenly started to speak, Oolaf tumbled off his chair. His mum screamed!

"Do not be afraid!" boomed the pot, splattering hot soup everywhere. "I have been sent by the gods to bring you news!"

Although Oolaf knew the gods sometimes brought things to life to send messages, he'd never heard of a talking pot before. "Forkbeard and the Vikings have been captured by Grellwig!" the pot boomed.

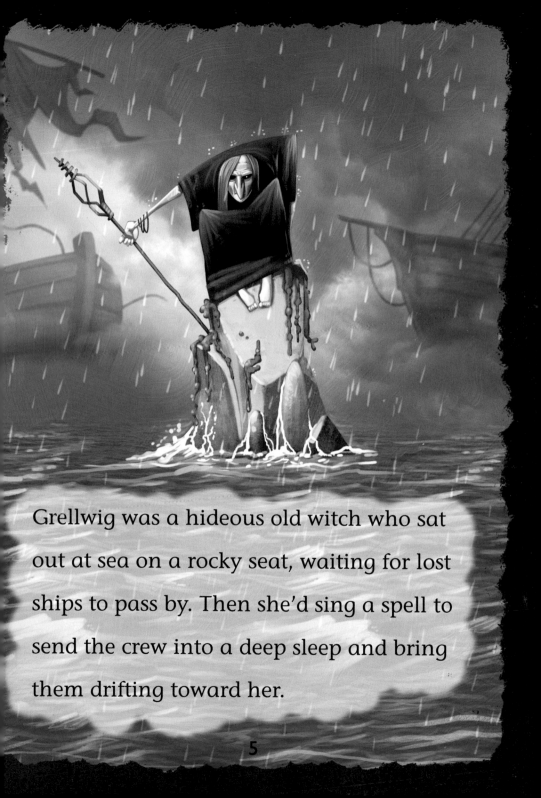

Grellwig was a hideous old witch who sat out at sea on a rocky seat, waiting for lost ships to pass by. Then she'd sing a spell to send the crew into a deep sleep and bring them drifting toward her.

"You must help them," wailed the pot, "or they'll be lost forever!"

"No man is safe from Grellwig's spells," said Oolaf's Mum, "but I know a brave Viking hero who would be safe ... because she's a girl."

"Bitra the Brave!" cried Oolaf.

"One more thing," shouted the pot as they raced off to find Bitra, "this soup needs more salt!"

Chapter Two

Bitra the Brave was practising her sword fighting. She was busy leaping and jumping all over the place, making it whistle and whizz above her head. Then she noticed Oolaf and his mum running down the hill.

She listened wide-eyed as they told her what the pot had said.

"I'll rescue them," Bitra promised.

"I'll help too," said Oolaf. "I'm not a man yet so Grellwig's spells can't hurt me either."

Oolaf's Mum didn't like the sound of that but Bitra promised to look after him.

She collected her sword, and Oolaf ran
back home to get the cooking pot.
"If anything can help us, this pot from
the gods can," he said.

Then they raced down to the shore
and boarded Bitra's little boat.

Chapter Three

After a while they came to a place where
the sea was flat and still. A grey mist crept
all around them, and crooked, black shapes
rose up from the depths. It was like a boat
graveyard.

"We're near," whispered Bitra. They paddled
silently between the wrecks and kept a
lookout for Forkbeard.

There were vessels of all shapes and sizes.
From each one came the soft snoring
of men caught under Grellwig's spell.

Oolaf soon spotted his father's ship. He saw his father, Forkbeard, slumped over the side, sleeping like a baby.

Ogbad the Good, Erik the Strong, Agnar the Smelly and MacMoonie the Lost were all fast asleep, too. No matter how hard Bitra and Oolaf tried, they couldn't wake them up.

They paddled off in search of Grellwig.
"Look, there she is!" cried Oolaf. He and
Bitra ducked down and peeked over the side
of their boat. Through the mist, a black
shape was perched on top of a slime-covered
rock. In one hand the witch held a magic
shell, and in the other a long, iron staff.

Chapter Four

As soon as she spied Bitra's boat, Grellwig put the shell to her thin lips and began singing in the most beautiful voice Oolaf had ever heard.

'Cross salty foam and bubbling sea,

sailor, sailor, come to me.

Drop those oars and breathe in deep,

forget your cares and fall asleep.

"A girl and a little boy," she grumbled,

realising her spell was powerless over them.

"You're so far away. Come closer, so I can

take a better look."

Bitra paddled nearer. Grellwig gave a cackle and wiggled her bony fingers over the sea. Long clumps of seaweed magically rose up and wound around the boat.

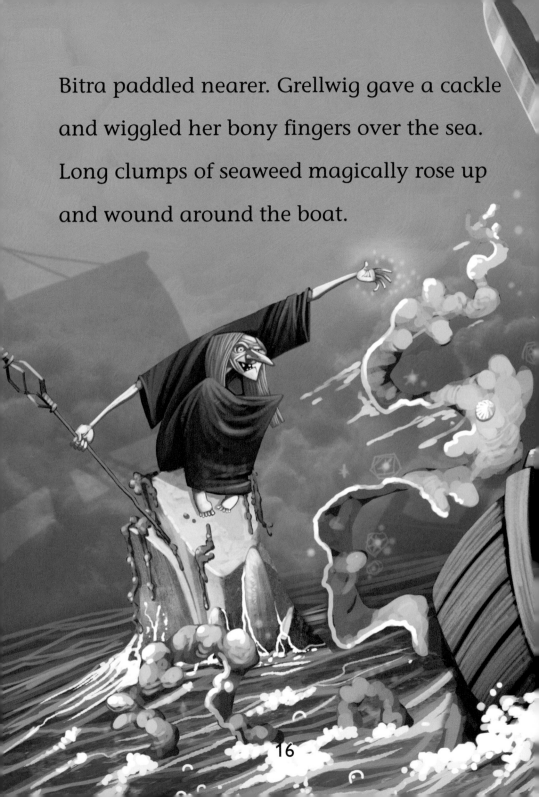

Bitra hacked away at the enchanted seaweed with her sword, but each time she cut some away, more grew back to pull the boat down.

Oolaf quickly grabbed the pot and tipped
the last of the hot soup all over it.

"HISS," went the seaweed, and disappeared
back into the sea.

"You'll have to do better than that, Grellwig,"
said Bitra.

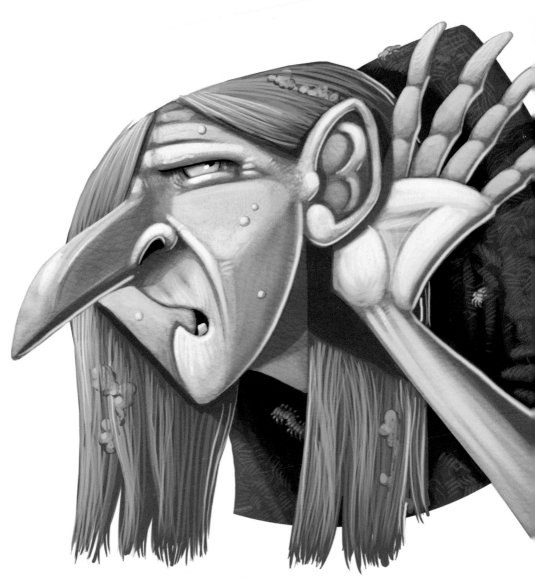

"I can't hear you," complained the witch.

"Come closer."

So Bitra paddled even nearer.

Grellwig then pulled a short rope out from
her sleeve. She knotted it, once, twice, three
times and held it up above her head.

Raindrops the size of pebbles began
thundering down from the sky, filling the
boat with water right up to the top.

Taking the pot from Oolaf, Bitra began scooping water as fast as she could. The pot coughed and spluttered but soon the boat was empty again. Bitra turned and gave the witch a big, bold stare.

Grellwig's face wrinkled like a rotten turnip. "You must be tired," Grellwig said. "Come and have a rest by me." Bitra paddled nearer still. Grellwig suddenly thrust the tip of her staff into the sea and started to stir.

The water began to swirl. Bitra's boat went round and round in circles, making her and Oolaf feel terribly dizzy.

"We need an anchor!" cried Oolaf.
He tied some rope around the pot and
threw it into the sea. "Hold on!" said the pot
as it sank to the bottom. The rope pulled
tight and the boat stopped spinning.
It sat bobbing gently on the waves.

Chapter Five

By now Grellwig was furious. She screeched and wailed, making such a noise that her spell began to break. She lifted the shell to sing, but she dropped it onto the rocks and it broke into a thousand pieces.

By now, the sleeping sailors began to stir. She tried singing without the shell but the ghastly noise that came out of her mouth just made everyone wake up quicker. Angry sailors' voices filled the air. Sails unfurled, oars hit water, and vessels of every shape and size drew nearer to the witch.

"Stop!" she shrieked. "Don't come any closer!" Then she stood up, something she had not done in a very long time! She wobbled on the slippery rock and hadn't noticed Bitra and Oolaf had paddled all the way up to her.

"Are we close enough now?" asked Bitra. She hurled the cooking pot at the witch. "Take that!" shouted Bitra. The pot hit Grellwig and knocked her off her feet. She fell backwards and plunged beneath the waves, never to be seen again.

There was a great cheer from all the ships.

"When we return home, we'll have a huge feast to celebrate our heroes, Oolaf and Bitra," promised Forkbeard.

"And from now we'll call you B*itra, the bravest of them all!*"

Then every longship and little boat escaped to the open sea, and the sailors had a great story to tell.

Meanwhile the cooking pot floated away as fast as it could. "I am never helping anyone again," it grumbled to itself.

Viking myths in the story

Talking pot

Vikings believed that the Norse Gods would often enchant objects, or come to Earth themselves in the shape of talking animals or in disguise.

Volva

The name Vikings gave to witches and enchantresses.

Grellwig's seat

Vikings believed that Norse witches sat on the top of high, decorated seats.

Grellwig's staff

Vikings thought that witches carried iron staffs. Graves of Norse Witches have been discovered complete with iron staffs that has been bent in half, to stop any power it might have had.

Grellwig's short rope

A witch tied knots in rope to control the weather.